BIBLE HEROES COLLECTION: DANIEL

published by Gold 'n' Honey Books
a part of the Questar publishing family

©1996 by Questar Publishers, Inc.
Illustrations ©1996 by Nan Brooks
Design by David Uttley (D² DesignWorks)

International Standard Book Number: 1-57673-014-X

Printed in the United States of America

For information:
QUESTAR PUBLISHERS, INC. · POST OFFICE BOX 1720 · SISTERS, OREGON 97759

96 97 98 99 00 01 02 03 — 10 9 8 7 6 5 4 3 2 1

DANIEL

A Boy Who Trusted God

BY MARLEE ALEX

ILLUSTRATIONS BY NAN BROOKS

Gold 'n' Honey BOOKS

PALACE PRISONERS

Far away and long ago,
in a place called Babylon,
there was a king named Nebuchadnezzar.
His mighty army fought against
the Israelites and won.

Nebuchadnezzar stole gold and
silver from God's temple. He also stole
young boys from their families.

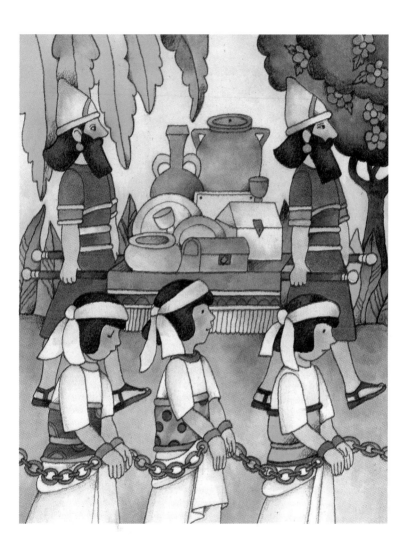

He made these boys work in his palace.
Among them was a boy named Daniel,
and three of his friends.

The king wanted the stolen boys
to forget their homes and become
just like the people in Babylon.
They would have to eat the same food,
read the same books,
and speak the same way that he did.
Worst of all, the king wanted
them to worship the gold statues and
wooden gods of Babylon.

"Eat!" said the guard.
"Your food is just like the king's."

But Daniel didn't want to do
what the guard asked.
"May I please eat something else?"
he asked politely.

"No!" said the guard.
"You'll get skinny and weak.
Then the king will cut off my head."

"Please," Daniel said.
"Try this for just ten days: Give me and
my friends vegetables and water.
Then see for yourself how we look."

"All right," said the guard.

The soldiers were afraid they would get
into trouble for changing the food.
But after they saw how strong and healthy
Daniel and his friends looked,
the soldiers let Daniel have his way.

BAD DREAMS

Three years later, King Nebuchadnezzar
gave the boys a big test.
Daniel and his friends did better
than everyone else.
"Good work, Daniel!" said the king.
"You and your friends Hananiah,
Mishael, and Azariah
will be my own special servants."

King Nebuchadnezzar
started having very bad dreams.
So he called together all of his
fortune-tellers, magicians, and wizards.
"What do you want us to do?" they asked.

"Tell me what I have dreamed
and explain what my dream means!"
demanded the king.
"I will give you many gifts.
But if you can't explain my dream—
I'll have you torn apart!
I'll tear down your houses, too!"

The wizards said,
"All right. Tell us your dream, O King!
Then we will tell you what it means."

But the king said,
"No! First, *you* must tell *me* what I dreamed.
Anyone can lie and pretend to know
what my dream means!"

All the magicians cried out,
"But *no one* can do that!"

"Then you will all be killed!"
raged the king.

The soldiers went to see Daniel.
"Give me an appointment with the king,"
Daniel said. "God will show me how
to explain the king's dream."

Daniel asked his friends to pray.
"God will help you," they said.
That night God showed Daniel
the king's dream.

Daniel told the king,
"There is a God who explains secret things.
This God wants to show you what
is going to happen."
Daniel described the dream.
Everything was exactly
as Nebuchadnezzar had seen it.

Then Daniel explained what the
dream meant. The king fell right onto
his face at Daniel's feet.
"You are the wisest man in Babylon!"
he said. "Now I know that your God
is the greatest god!"

Nebuchadnezzar told Daniel,
"You will be a ruler in my kingdom.
I am putting you in charge of
all the wise men."

"Can my friends be rulers, too?"
Daniel asked.

"Why, certainly,"
said the king with a wide smile.
"But only you will live in the palace!"

A Proud King

A few months
later Nebuchadnezzar forgot everything
he had learned about God.
The king built a giant gold statue.
He ordered everyone
to worship the statue instead of
the one true God.

Then Nebuchadnezzar had another
scary dream. He called for Daniel right away.
"Describe my dream,"
he commanded, "and explain it to me."
Daniel was frightened by the king's dream.
He didn't want to tell the king bad news.
But Nebuchadnezzar said,
"Just tell me what you see."

"You'll live among wild animals,"
Daniel told the king.
"You'll eat grass for seven years,
until you learn that God is ruler
over every king on earth.
Please take my advice, O King," Daniel said.
"Stop sinning and do what is right."

King Nebuchadnezzar thought awhile
about what Daniel had said.
But he soon forgot God's warning to him.
A year later, he was walking on the flat roof
of his palace, under the stars.
"This all shows how great I am," he thought.

Suddenly a voice spoke from heaven:
"Proud King Nebuchadnezzar,
your power is taken away.
You must live among wild animals.
You will learn that the Most High God
rules over every king."

The words Nebuchadnezzar
heard came true. In the desert, his hair
grew long like feathers.
His nails grew out like the claws of a bird.
At the end of seven years,
the king admitted,
"Daniel was right. God humbled me."

WRITING ON A WALL

Soon Nebuchadnezzar's son, Belshazzar, became the new king. One night he had a big party. He served wine in the same gold and silver cups his father had stolen from God's temple years before.

Belshazzar and his guests laughed and bragged about their riches. They praised their little pretend gods that they had made out of wood and stone.

Suddenly, giant fingers appeared beside
the wall! The fingers started writing
something on the plaster. The king and his
guests watched, shaking with fear.

Belshazzar called for
his magicians and wizards.
"Tell me, what is the meaning of this?"
he demanded. But none of the wise men
could explain the writing. The king and
his guests were scared and confused.

Then King Belshazzar's mother said,
"Don't be afraid. I know a man named
Daniel who may understand."

So Daniel was brought to the king.
"Tell me what this writing means,"
Belshazzar ordered.

Daniel began to explain the writing.
"Your father was a powerful king.
But he became proud and stubborn.
So God took his throne and crown away.
You already know this.
But you've done wrong anyway.
You have angered God by using cups
from His temple as you praise
your pretend gods!"

And that very night, Belshazzar died.

No Praying Allowed

A man named Darius
became the new king of Babylon.
Darius put Daniel in charge of the kingdom's
governors. "You'll share this work with
two other men," he said.
Their job was to make sure the governors
didn't cheat the king.

"Daniel, I'm very pleased with your hard work!" the king said one morning. "I'm putting you in charge of everyone." This made the other two men very angry!

The two angry men planned trouble for Daniel. "You are so great," they flattered King Darius. "Make a new law saying that for thirty days no one may pray to any god but you, O King. Anyone who doesn't obey must be thrown into the lions' den!" The king did what the men asked.

Now, Daniel had always prayed three
times a day to the one true God.
"Nothing will ever change that," he thought.
"I will always pray to God,
no matter what!"
So, that morning, as always, Daniel
folded his hands and prayed to God.
The two angry, jealous men
went to Daniel's home.
There they saw Daniel praying
at the window.

"King Darius!"
they shouted, running back to the palace.
"Don't you have a law against praying to
other gods, a law which can't be canceled?"

"Yes," said Darius.

"Well," they said, "Daniel is not keeping
your law. He still prays to his
God three times a day."

King Darius realized he'd been tricked.
"Throw Daniel to the lions,"
he ordered. Then he sent a message to
Daniel. "May your God save you!" it said.

DANIEL
AND THE LIONS

The lions were pacing their cave
when the soldiers arrived
with Daniel. The huge cats hadn't
eaten all day.
"Stop your roaring," one soldier yelled.
"You'll get your dinner soon enough!"

The soldiers grabbed Daniel and threw him
into the den of lions. Then they rolled a big
rock over the entrance. King Darius himself
put his seal on the entrance.

The king could not eat that evening
or sleep at all that long night. He kept
thinking about Daniel.
Early the next morning
the king hurried to the lions' cave.
Everything was very quiet.
"Daniel!" shouted Darius as loud as he could.
"Daniel! Has your God saved you?"

Then Darius heard a cheerful voice:
"My God sent his angel," Daniel said,
"who closed the lions' mouths.
They have not hurt me.
My God knows that I am innocent.
I did nothing wrong to you, my king."

A big smile broke out on the king's face.
He took the seal off the rock.
"Lift Daniel out!" he ordered his soldiers.
When they did, everyone stared, amazed.
Daniel did not have one scratch on him.
He smiled at the peaceful lions.

The king was very angry at the men
who had tricked him. He ordered that *they*
be thrown to the lions!
As the men fell down, the animals grabbed
them before they had even hit the ground.

Then King Darius made a new law.
"The God of Daniel is great," the law said.
"Everyone must worship the living God,
who rules forever!"

Daniel lived to be a very old man.
God spoke to him about the future
in many dreams.
To this day, people all over the
world read and study Daniel's
dreams in the Bible.

BIBLE LESSON

Daniel was a hero because he believed in God—
no matter what!